Little Penguin
The Emperor of Antarctica

by **Jonathan London**   illustrated by **Julie Olson**

Marshall Cavendish Children

All rights reserved
Marshall Cavendish Corporation
99 White Plains Road
Tarrytown, NY 10591
www.marshallcavendish.us/kids

Library of Congress Cataloging-in-Publication Data
London, Jonathan
Little penguin : the Emperor of Antarctica / by Jonathan
London; illustrated by Julie Olson. — 1st ed.
p. cm.
Summary: In Antarctica, Little Emperor grows from a
hatchling who depends on his parents for food and
warmth, to an adult, ready to live in the sea on his own.
ISBN 978-0-7614-5954-5 (hardcover)
ISBN 978-0-7614-6062-6 (ebook)
1. Emperor penguin—Juvenile fiction. [1. Emperor penguin—
Fiction. 2. Penguins—Fiction. 3. Animals—Infancy—Fiction.
4. Parental behavior in animals—Fiction. 5. Antarctica—
Fiction.] I. Olson, Julie, 1976— ill. II. Title.
PZ10.3.L8534Lh 2011   [E]—dc22   2010026501

The illustrations were rendered in pencil, watercolor,
and digital media.
Book design by Vera Soki
Editors: Nathalie Le Du and Robin Benjamin

Printed in China (E)
First edition
10 9 8 7 6 5 4 3 2 1

mc **Marshall Cavendish**
Children

For Margery C., Barbara, Leah, and sweet Maureen
—J.L.

To my littlest emperor, Archer
—J.O.

When the Little Emperor of Antarctica
crawled out of his cracked egg,
he looked around with his wobbly head.

He was cradled on his father's feet!

Little Emperor was cold and hungry.
Feed me! Feed me! he peeped.

Father Penguin dripped crop "milk" into the chick's wide-open mouth.

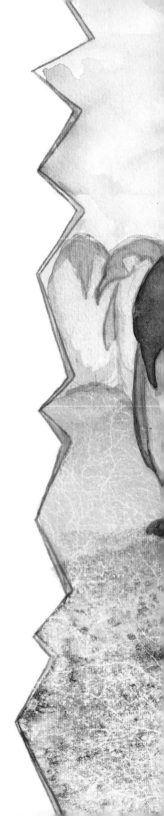

Then he tucked the chick under his belly flap.
Now Little Emperor was cozy and warm.

But soon he was hungry again,
and Father Penguin was out of milk.
Little Emperor whistled and peeped
and poked his head out. *Feed me! Feed me!*

Just in time, Mother Penguin
crooned her song across the windblown ice!
Father Penguin trumpeted back.
Here! We're here!

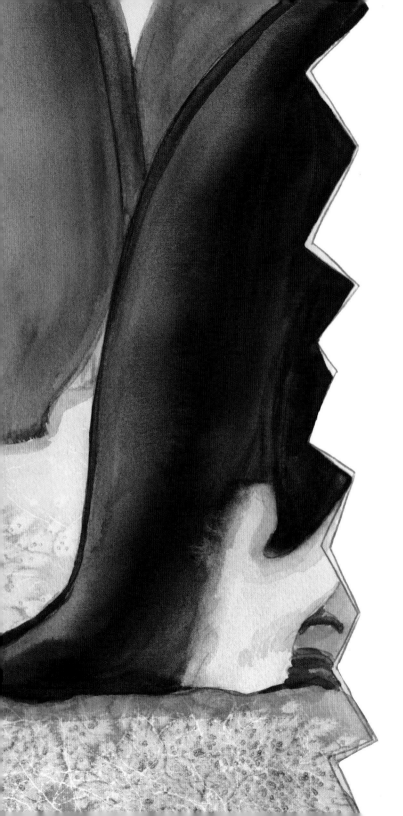

There! Among thousands of voices,
she recognized the call of her mate!
She had been away for three months—
hunting in the open sea—
and now she had made the long trek back . . .

and her belly was filled to bursting
with fish, squid, and krill for her chick.

Famished, Little Emperor nestled between her feet
and jammed his bill deep inside his mother's beak—
and ate and ate and ate.

With a full belly, Little Emperor took his first tentative step. . . .

Whoops!

He stumbled and slipped
on the ice.
Then he stood up, dazed
and bewildered . . .
and tried again.

Tired, he snuggled into the soft
comfort of his mother's belly flap
and peeked back out at his father.

Peekaboo!

But Father Penguin was starving!
While Mother Penguin had been away,
he had stood in a huddle
with the other males—
each balancing a single egg—
and hadn't eaten for three whole months!

Now it was *his* turn to make
the long, hard journey
down to the sea for food.

And for weeks at a time,
through the long night of winter,
Little Emperor's father and mother
took turns trudging back and forth,
back and forth, sharing their catch
with their chick.

And all this time, Little Emperor
grew and grew.

By the time the sun came back,
spreading its light like a giant wing
across the gleaming ice,
Little Emperor was living more and more
with the other young penguins.

With his soft tuft of down
sprouting like wild grass,
Little Emperor played with the others . . .
and waited for the sea ice to open,
not so far away.

At last, in midsummer, it was time!
At five months old,
Little Emperor and his clan
waddled down to the sea.

They hopped . . .
and leaped . . .
and tobogganed . . .

WHOOSH!

until they reached the ocean.

Curious and scared,
Little Emperor craned his neck
and looked out to sea
at the floating castles of ice.

Suddenly, another young
penguin bumped him!
He slipped . . .

and plunged in—*SPLOOSH!*—
and dove underwater.

Soon the water foamed and boiled
with hundreds of little penguins
flashing through the sea.

But something was lurking.
Something was waiting. . . .

A ferocious leopard seal!

Little Emperor spun and twirled.
He torpedoed away . . .

leaped like a dolphin . . .

and rocketed clear out of the sea,
escaping the seal's deadly jaws—

SNAP!

Squawking an alarm,
Little Emperor waddled
along the ice edge . . .

till the leopard of the sea
was gone.

Safe now, he plunged back in,
paddling and leaping
through the thawing ocean—
chasing fish and squid and krill—
bursting with energy and life.

Now the Little Emperor of Antarctica
would live at sea. In four years,
as the dark of winter approached,
he would begin the ancient journey
back to the breeding grounds . . .

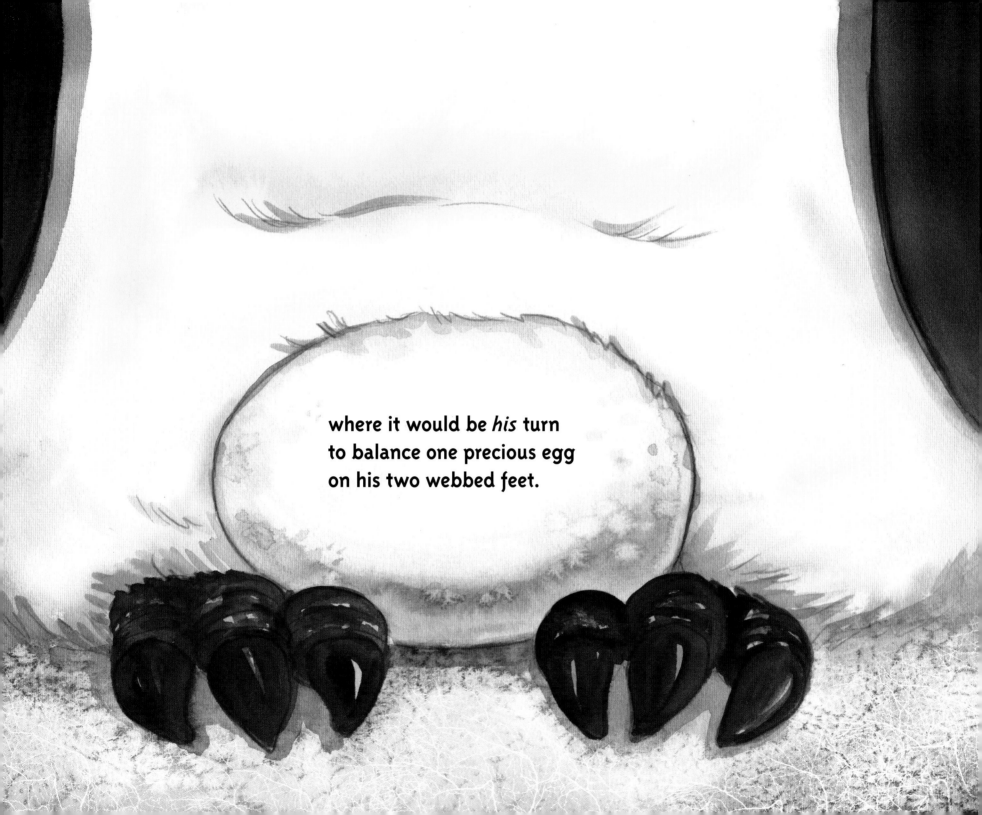

where it would be *his* turn
to balance one precious egg
on his two webbed feet.

Author's Note

The penguins in this story are the emperor penguins. These regal birds are the aristocrats of Antarctica. They are the biggest of all the penguins, standing four feet tall and weighing up to ninety-nine pounds.

Living on the coastal ice of Antarctica, the emperor penguin survives in extremely harsh weather. Gathering in the Antarctic autumn (late March through May), the emperors mate and lay their eggs. Unlike other birds, the mother transfers the egg to the father and he incubates the egg for sixty-four days, through the height of winter. The father feeds the chick with crop milk—a thick, nourishing, creamy substance that develops in the male's crop, or gullet. As the fierce winds howl across the ice, the mother trudges, perhaps 100 miles, to the open sea to hunt. By the time she returns to the breeding colony, the father will have lost half his body weight. Although the emperors don't mate for life, a couple remains together while breeding and raising its young.

The chicks grow quickly. Their biggest danger, while living on the ice, comes from giant petrels, which bombard them with their sharp beaks.

In the eternal daylight of summer, when the sea ice breaks open and the fledglings' adult feathers have grown in, the young penguins go to the sea for the first time, where their main predator is the 900-pound leopard seal. But the young, flightless birds learn to swim quickly, flying underwater, diving to depths of more than 1,700 feet, the deepest of any bird.

For the next four years, the young penguins, with their solid bones and thick blubber, live at sea. Then as the polar darkness returns, they make the long journey back to their breeding grounds, and the ancient cycle begins again.

Though these beautiful birds are not yet listed as endangered, scientists fear that if global warming continues, the majestic emperors of Antarctica may be close to extinction within the next 100 years.